For Pauline, exquisite equestrian and loyal friend of all creatures,
two-footed and four-footed—S.J.

Text copyright © 1986 by Random House, Inc. Pictures copyright © 1986 by Susan Jeffers. All rights reserved under International and Pan-American Copyright Conventions. Published in the
United States by Random House, Inc., New York, and simultaneously in Canada by Random House of Canada Limited, Toronto.
Library of Congress Cataloging in Publication Data: McKinley, Robin. Black Beauty. SUMMARY: A horse in nineteenth-century England recounts his experiences with both good and bad masters.
1. Children's stories, English. 2. Horses—Juvenile fiction. [1. Horses—Fiction] I. Sewell, Anna, 1820–1878. II. Jeffers, Susan, ill. III. Title. PZ10.3.M455Bl 1986 [Fic] 84-27575
ISBN: 0-394-86575-8 (trade); 0-394-96575-2 (lib. bdg.)
Manufactured in the United States of America   1   2   3   4   5   6   7   8   9   0

BLACK BEAUTY

By Anna Sewell
Adapted by Robin McKinley
Pictures by Susan Jeffers

Random House · New York

The first place I remember is a large pleasant meadow, where I lived with my mother. As soon as I was old enough to eat grass, my mother used to go out to work in the daytime and come back in the evening. Our master was a good, kind man, and we were fond of him.

One day, when I was still quite young, I heard the cry of dogs. "They have found a hare," said my mother, "and if it comes this way, we shall see the hunt."

A hare wild with fright rushed by; then came the dogs, who leaped over the brook below our meadow. After them came men and women on horseback. The hare tried to get through the fence around our meadow; but it was too late, and the dogs were upon her. Two horses were down by the brook. One of the riders was getting out of the water covered with mud; the other lay still. It was Squire Gordon's only son, and his neck was broken. The farrier came to look at the horses; he shook his head over the one, for he had a broken leg. Someone came with a gun; there was a loud bang and the black horse moved no more.

Not many days after, we heard the church bell tolling for a long time; they were carrying young Gordon to the churchyard to bury him. What they did with the black horse, I never knew; but 'twas all for one little hare.

By the time I was four years old, I had grown quite handsome. My coat was a bright black, and I had one white foot and a white star on my forehead. My master decided it was time to break me in.

Breaking in means to teach a horse to wear a saddle and bridle and to carry a rider on his back. He has also to learn to wear a collar and

harness and to have a cart or carriage fixed behind him so that he drags it after him. He must learn to go quietly and just as his rider or driver wishes. He must have no will of his own, but always do his master's will, even though he may be very tired or hungry. So breaking in is very important.

I had been used to a halter, but now I was to have a bit and bridle. After a good deal of coaxing, my master got the bit into my mouth. I did not care for it, but I wished to please my master. Next came the saddle, but that was not so bad. And one morning my master got on my back and rode me round the meadow on the soft grass. I felt rather proud to carry my master.

Next my master went with me to the smith's forge, where the blacksmith took a piece of iron the shape of my foot, clapped it on, and drove some nails through the shoe into my hoof. But this did not hurt me, and I stood still on three legs till he had done them all. My feet felt very stiff and heavy, but in time I got used to it.

Now my master broke me to harness: first the collar; then the bridle with sidepieces called blinkers against my eyes, so that I could only see straight in front of me; and then a small saddle with a nasty stiff strap that went under my tail—that was the crupper.

My master often drove me in double harness with my mother. She told me that the better I behaved, the better I should be treated. "But," she said, "there are many kinds of men: some are good and thoughtful like our master, but there are also bad, cruel men and foolish, careless men. A horse never knows who may buy him, but you have been well bred and well trained, and I hope you will always be gentle and do your work with a good will."

Squire Gordon decided to buy me, and a man came and took me away to the town of Birtwick, where the squire and his family lived. Squire Gordon's park was entered by a large iron gate, and then there was a smooth road between large old trees; then another gate to the house, which was called the hall, and beyond that the orchard and stables. I was put in a fine large loose box, and when I looked around, I saw in the stall next to mine a little fat gray pony. I said, "How do you do? What is your name?"

He turned round as far as his halter would allow, for the other stalls were not loose boxes like mine, but straight stalls, where the horse is tied up. "My name is Merrylegs. I carry the young ladies on my back, and they think a great deal of me, and so does James, the stable boy. Are you going to live in the box?"

Just then a horse's head looked over from the stall beyond Merrylegs's; the ears were laid back, and the eye looked ill-tempered. This was a tall, handsome chestnut mare. She looked at me and said, "So it is you who have turned me out of my box."

"I beg your pardon," I said. "I have turned no one out; the man who bought me put me here."

In the afternoon, when the mare went out, Merrylegs told me: "Ginger bites. When she was in the loose box, she used to bite and snap very much, and so my young ladies were afraid to come into the stable, and I missed them very much. I hope they will now come again, if you do not bite."

I told him I never bit anything but my food and could not think what pleasure Ginger found it.

"I don't think she does find pleasure in it," said Merrylegs. "It's just a bad habit. She says no one was ever kind to her and why should she not bite? But I think she might be good-tempered here, for John Manly, our coachman, does all he can to please her, and you never saw such a kind boy as James."

The next morning the squire came to try me. I found that he was a very good rider and thoughtful of his horse too. When we came home, Mrs. Gordon asked, "How do you like him, my dear?"

"A pleasanter animal I could not wish to mount," he replied. "What shall we call him?"

"He really is quite a beauty, and he has such a sweet, good-tempered face and a fine, intelligent eye—what do you say to calling him Black Beauty?"

"Black Beauty—why, yes, I think that is a very good name."

A few days after my first ride with the squire, I went out with Ginger in the carriage. I wondered how we should get on together; but except for laying her ears back when I was led up to her, she behaved very well. She did her work honestly, and I could not wish to have a better partner in double harness; John Manly had more often to hold us in than to urge us forward. After we had been out two or three times together, we grew quite friendly.

Sometimes on fine Sundays we were turned out in the paddock or the old orchard. We galloped, or lay down, or rolled over on our backs, or nibbled the sweet grass, just as we liked; and we talked. One day I told Ginger about my bringing up and breaking in.

"Well," said she, "if I had had your bringing up, I might have had as good a temper as you, but it has all been so different with me. The man that had the care of us young colts did not ill-use us, but he did not care for us one bit further than to see that we had plenty to eat. When it came to breaking in, several men cornered me, and one caught me by the nose and held it so tight I could hardly draw my breath. Another took my jaw in his hard hand and wrenched my mouth open, and so forced the bit into my mouth. And this was my first experience of men.

"The old master was a gentle man, but he had given up the trade to his son, who was a strong, hard man who used to boast that he had never found a horse that could throw him. He worked me as hard as he could, and at night I lay down tired and miserable and angry. One morning he came for me early, with a saddle and bridle and new kind of bit. He had only just mounted when something I did put him out of temper, and he pulled hard on the rein. The new bit was very painful, and I reared up, which angered him still more, and he began to beat me. I kicked and plunged as I had never done before. For a long time

he stuck to the saddle and hurt me cruelly with his whip and spurs, but after a terrible struggle I threw him off and galloped to the other end of the field. The sun was very hot, and the flies settled on my bleeding flanks. I was hungry, but there was no grass in that field; I wanted to rest, but with the saddle strapped on tightly, there was no comfort; and there was not a drop of water to drink.

"At last, as the sun went down, the old master came out with a sieve of oats in his hand. I stood still and let him come up, for his voice took all my fear away. He patted me while I ate the oats, and the blood on my sides seemed to anger him. He led me to the stable; just at the door stood his son, and I laid my ears back and snapped at him. 'Stand back,' said his father. 'You've done a bad day's work for this filly. You've not yet learned your trade, for a bad-tempered man will never make a good-tempered horse.'

"After my breaking in," Ginger went on, "I was bought by a fashionable gentleman to make up a team. We were driven with a bearing rein, and I hated it worse than anything, for it holds your head up very high, and you are not able to move it except with a jerk still higher, and your neck aches till you do not know how to bear it. And you have two bits instead of one; and mine was a sharp one, and hurt my tongue, but if I fretted the whip was laid on. My master only thought we looked spirited and stylish. I grew more and more restless and irritable—I could not help it—and I began to snap and kick when anyone came to harness me; for this the groom beat me. One day, as they had just buckled us into the carriage and were straining my head up with that rein, I began to kick and rear. I broke a lot of harness; and that was the end of that place.

"Of course, it is very different here, and they seem to be kind, and they do not use the bearing rein; but who knows how long it will last? I wish I could think about things as you do, but I can't after all I have gone through."

I was sorry for Ginger, but as the weeks went on she grew much more gentle and cheerful and lost her watchful, wary look. "She'll be as good as Black Beauty soon," said John. "Kindness is all the medicine she wants, poor thing!"

I grew very fond of John, he was so gentle and kind. When he cleaned me, he knew the tender and ticklish places; when he brushed my head, he went as carefully over my eyes as if they were his own. James, the stable boy, was just as gentle and pleasant in his way, and I knew myself, and Ginger and Merrylegs and the others, to be well off in this happy place.

One day late in the autumn my master had a journey to make on business. I was harnessed to the cart, and John went with his master. There had been a great deal of rain, and now the wind was very high. We went along merrily till we came to the low wooden bridge. The man at the tollgate said the river was rising fast.

When we got to the town, the master's business kept him a long time. We did not start for home till late in the afternoon, and by the time we got to the bridge, it was nearly dark. We could just see at the bank that the water was very high. We were going along at a good pace, but the moment my feet touched the bridge, I felt sure there was something wrong. I dared not go forward, and I stopped dead. "Go on, Beauty," said my master, and he gave me a touch with the whip, but I would not stir.

Just then the man at the tollgate on the other side ran up waving a torch. "Halloo! Stop!" he cried. "The bridge is broken in the middle; if you come on you'll be into the river."

"Dear God!" said my master, and he gently turned me to the road by the riverside, but we had to go a long way to the next bridge. When we came at last to the park gates, the gardener was looking out for us. He said that the mistress had been worried, fearing some accident; and as we came up to the hall, the mistress ran out, saying, "Are you really safe, my dear?"

"We are safe; but if your Black Beauty had not been wiser than we were, we should all have been carried down the river."

My master and mistress decided to pay a visit to some friends who lived at a distance from our home, and James was to drive them there, instead of John, the coachman; for James was soon to go to a new place, to work for a friend of the master's. The master had promised to give James practice at driving before he left.

Just as the sun was going down we reached the town where we were to spend the night. We stopped at a large hotel. James stood by while Ginger and I were rubbed down and given our grain, and then he and the hostler who had taken care of us left the stable together.

I cannot say how long I slept, but I woke up in the night feeling very uncomfortable. I heard Ginger coughing, and the other horses moved restlessly. It was quite dark, and the stable was full of smoke. I listened and heard a soft rushing noise and a low crackling, and there was a red light flickering at the open hayloft door.

The next thing I heard was James's voice, quiet and cheery as it always was. I stood nearest the door, so he came to me first: "Beauty, on with your bridle." With him near me, indeed I had no fear; and patting me soothingly, he led me out of the stable. When we were safe in the yard, he shouted, "Here, somebody! Take this horse while I go back for the other."

There was much confusion in the yard as the other horses were led out and the carriages and gigs were pulled free; but above the din I heard a loud, clear voice, which I knew was my master's: "James Howard! Are you there?" There was no answer, but I heard a crash within the stable, and the fire roared up, and then I gave a loud joyful neigh as I saw James coming through the smoke leading Ginger. She was coughing violently, and he was not able to speak.

"My brave lad!" said our master.

The rest of our journey was very easy; we stopped for two or three days with the friends of our master and mistress, and then returned home. We were glad to be in our own stable again, and John was glad to see us. James asked, "Do you know who is coming in my place?"

"Little Joe Green," said John.

"Joe Green! Why, he's a child!"

"He is fourteen and a half," said John, "and he is willing and kind-hearted, and I know the master would like to give him the chance. I was only as old as Joe when my father and mother died of the fever; and the master took me into the stable under the coachman that was here then. I am not the man to turn up his nose at a little boy."

One night, a few days after James had left, I was roused from sleep by the ringing of the stable bell. I heard John run up to the hall from his little cottage near the stable; and then he was back again, calling out, "Wake up, Beauty, you must go your best tonight." He took me at a quick trot up to the hall door, where the squire stood with a lamp in his hand.

"Ride for your mistress's life, John," he said.

John said, "Yes, sir." The gardener was ready with the gate open, and away we went through the park and through the village. I don't believe that my grandfather who won the big race at Newmarket could have gone faster. The church clock struck three as we drew up at

27

Dr. White's door. John rang the bell twice, and Dr. White, in his nightshirt, looked out the window and said, "What do you want?"

"Mrs. Gordon is very ill, sir; master thinks she will die if you cannot get there."

"I will come," he said. He was soon at the door. "My horse has been out all day and is tired. May I have your horse?"

John stroked my neck; I was very hot. "Take care of him, sir." In a moment we had left John far behind.

Joe was at the gate; my master was at the hall door, and the doctor went into the house with him, and Joe led me to the stable. I was glad to get home; my legs shook under me, and I could only stand and pant, and I steamed all over. Poor Joe! As yet he knew very little; but he did the best he knew. He rubbed my legs and chest, but he did not put my warm cloth on me; he thought I was so hot I should not like it. Then he gave me cold water to drink, and some hay and grain, and thinking he had done right, he went away. Soon I began to tremble, and turned deadly cold. My legs and chest ached, and I felt sore all over. I wished for John, but he had eight miles to walk, so I lay down in my straw. After a long while I heard John at the door, and I gave a low moan, for I was in great pain. He was at my side in a moment. He covered me with two or three warm cloths; he made me some warm gruel, which I drank; and then I went to sleep, but not before I heard John say, "Stupid boy! No cloth put on, and I dare say the water was cold too."

I was now very ill, and I could not draw my breath without pain. John nursed me night and day, and my master, too, often came to see me. "My poor Beauty," he said one day, "my good horse, you saved your mistress's life!"

I do not know how long I was ill. I thought I should die, and I believe they all thought so too. One night John had to give me some medicine;

Joe's father, Thomas Green, came to help him. "I wish, John, you'd say a kind word to Joe; the boy is broken-hearted. He is not a bad boy."

John said slowly, "You must not be too hard on me, Tom. I know he meant no harm; but that horse is the pride of my heart, to say nothing of his being such a favorite with the master and mistress. To think that his life may be flung away in this manner is more than I can bear; but I will try to give the boy a good word tomorrow."

"Well, John! Thank you. I knew you did not wish to be too hard, and I am glad you see it was only ignorance."

John's voice startled me as he answered: "*Only* ignorance! Only *ignorance!* How can you talk about *only* ignorance! Don't you know that it is the worst thing in the world, next to wickedness? Which does the most mischief, heaven only knows. If people can say, 'Oh! I did not know, I did not mean any harm,' they think it is all right."

I heard no more of this conversation, for the medicine did well and sent me to sleep, and in the morning I felt much better. But I often thought of John's words when I came to know more of the world.

I had now lived in this happy place three years, but sad changes were about to come over us. We knew that our mistress was ill; the doctor was often at the house, and the master looked grave and anxious. Then we heard that she must leave her home and go to a warm country. The news fell upon the household like the tolling of a death bell. John went about his work silent and sad, and Joe no longer whistled.

Master sold Ginger and me to his old friend, the Earl of W—, for he thought we should have a good place there; Merrylegs he had given to the vicar on the condition that he should never be sold.

The last sad day had come; the heavy luggage had been sent off the day before, and most of the servants had left. Ginger and I brought the carriage up to the hall door for the last time, for the master and the mistress and the two young ladies, who were weeping bitterly.

When we reached the railway station, mistress said in her sweet voice, "Good-bye, John; God bless you." I felt the rein twitch, but John made no answer; perhaps he could not speak. Poor Joe stood close to our heads to hide his tears. Very soon the train came puffing into the station. In but a few minutes it had glided away again, leaving behind it only clouds of white smoke and some very heavy hearts.

The next morning Ginger and I were taken to Earlshall Park, where the Earl of W— lived. We were taken to a light, airy stable and placed in boxes next to each other. John said to our new coachman, Mr. York, "We have never used the bearing rein on either of these horses; the black horse never had one on, and the dealer said it was the gag bit that spoiled the other's temper."

"Well," said York, "if they come here, they must wear the bearing rein. I prefer a loose rein myself, and his lordship is very reasonable about horses; but it must be tight up when my lady drives."

"I am sorry for it, very sorry," said John. He came round to each of us for the last time; his voice sounded very sad.

York told the earl what John had said. "Well," said he, "you must keep an eye on the mare, and start with the bearing rein easy. I'll mention it to her ladyship."

In the afternoon we were harnessed and put to the carriage. This was my first time wearing a bearing rein, and though it certainly was a nuisance not to be able to get my head down now and then, it did not pull my head higher than I was accustomed to carrying it. The next

day at three o'clock we were again at the door of the earl's hall; and we heard her ladyship's silk dress rustle as she came down the steps, and in a haughty voice she said, "York, you must put those horses' heads higher."

York came round to our heads and shortened the rein, and then I began to understand what Ginger had told me. I had to pull with my head held up tightly now, and that took all the spirit out of me, and I felt the strain in my back and legs. When we came in, Ginger said, "Now you see what it is like, but this is not bad."

Day by day our bearing reins were shortened, and instead of looking forward with pleasure to having my harness put on, as I used to do, I began to dread it. Ginger, too, seemed restless, though she said very little.

One day my lady came down later than usual, and the silk rustled more than ever. "Are you never going to get those horses' heads up, York? Raise them at once."

York came to me first, while the groom stood at Ginger's head. He drew my head back and fixed the rein so tight that it was almost intolerable. Then he went to Ginger, who was impatiently jerking her head up and down against the bit, as was her way now. She had a good idea of what was coming, and the moment York unhooked the rein in order to shorten it, she reared up so suddenly that she struck York roughly in the face and knocked his hat off; the groom was nearly thrown down. At once they both jumped to her head, but she still plunged and kicked in a most desperate manner; at last she kicked right over the carriage pole and fell down.

The groom set me free from Ginger and the carriage and led me back to my box. He just turned me in as I was, and ran back, and there I stood, angry and sore, with my head still strained up by the rein attached to the small harness saddle and no power to get it down. Before long, however, Ginger, looking a good deal bruised, was led in by two grooms. York came with her, and then came to look at me, and he let down my head. "These bearing reins! Fashion, and no sense!" he said to himself. "I thought we should have some mischief soon."

Ginger was never put into the carriage again, but when she was well of her bruises, Lord George, one of the earl's younger sons, said he should like to have her; he was sure she would make a good hunter. I was still a carriage horse and had a fresh partner named Max. He had always been used to the tight rein, and I asked him how he stood it.

"Well," he said, "I stand it because I must, because people who know nothing of horses like the way we look with bearing reins on; but it is shortening my life, and it will shorten yours, too, if you have to go on wearing it."

What I suffered for four long months in my lady's carriage would be hard to describe; but I am sure that had it lasted much longer, either my health or my temper would have given away. My breathing grew painful, my neck and chest were sore and strained, and my mouth and tongue tender. I felt worn and depressed.

A man named Reuben Smith was left in charge of the stables when York went to London with the earl and his lady. No one understood his business better than Smith did, and when he was all right, there could not be a more valuable man. But he had one great fault, and that was the love of whisky. York had spoken about him to the earl, who was kind-hearted, and Smith had promised that he would never taste another drop as long as he lived at Earlshall.

One day Smith rode me to the town and ordered the hostler to have me ready for him again at six o'clock. A nail in one of my front shoes had started to come loose, but the hostler did not notice it till six o'clock. The man then told Smith and asked if he should have the shoe looked to.

"No," said Smith, "that will be all right till we get home." He spoke in a very offhand way, and it was unlike him not to see about a loose shoe; and yet he did not come for me at seven, nor at eight, and it was nearly nine o'clock before he called for me, and then it was with a loud, rough voice. Almost before we were out of town, he whipped me into a gallop, and went on whipping me, though I was going full speed. The moon had not yet risen, and it was very dark. The roads were stony, and as I went over them at this pace, my shoe became looser, and when we were near the turnpike gate, it came off. If Smith had been in his right senses, he would have noticed something wrong in my pace; but he was too drunk to notice anything.

Beyond the turnpike was a long piece of road, upon which fresh stones had just been laid, large, sharp stones over which no horse could go quickly without danger. Over this road, with one shoe gone, I was forced to gallop at my greatest speed, my rider meanwhile cutting me with his whip. Of course my shoeless foot suffered dreadfully; the hoof was broken and split down to the quick, and the inside was terribly cut by the sharpness of the stones.

No horse could keep his footing under such circumstances. I stumbled and fell heavily to my knees. Smith was flung off, and at the speed I had been going, he must have fallen very hard. I recovered my feet and limped to the side of the road. The moon had just risen, and by its light

I could see Smith lying a few yards beyond me. I could do nothing for him nor myself, and I listened hopefully for the sound of wheels or footsteps. It must have been nearly midnight when I heard the sound of a horse's feet. I neighed loudly and was overjoyed to hear an answering neigh from Ginger, and men's voices. They came slowly over the stones and stopped at the dark figure that lay upon the ground.

One of the men stooped over him. "It is Reuben!" he said.

"He's dead," said the other man solemnly.

"Why, the horse has been down and thrown him! Who would have thought the black horse would have done that? Nobody thought he could fall." He then attempted to lead me forward. I took a step, but almost fell again.

"He's bad in his foot as well as his knees. Look here—his hoof is cut all to pieces. He might well fall down, poor fellow! I'm afraid it has been the old thing with Reuben."

I shall never forget that night's walk home; it was more than three miles. I was led slowly, and I limped on as well as I could. At last I reached my own box, and the next day the farrier examined my knees. He said that I was not spoiled for work, but that I would never lose the scars.

While my knees healed, I was turned into a small meadow for a month or two. I was all alone, and though I enjoyed the sweet grass, I felt very lonely. Ginger and I had become fast friends, and I particularly missed her. Then one morning my pasture gate was opened, and who should come in but dear old Ginger.

We were glad to meet, but it was not for our pleasure that she was turned out with me. She had been strained by hard riding and now was to be given a long rest. Lord George, the earl's son, would hunt and race whenever he could get the chance, quite careless of his horse. Ginger's wind was touched, besides which he was too heavy for her, and her back was injured. "And so," she said, "here we are—ruined in our prime—you by a drunkard and I by a fool. It is very hard."

One day the earl came into the meadow, and York was with him. The earl was angry. "What I care most for is that these horses of my old friend, who thought they would find a good home with me, are ruined. The mare shall have a year's rest, but the black one must be sold. 'Tis a great pity, but I will not have knees like that in my stable."

York said, "I know a man who is master of some livery stables. He often wants a good horse at a low price, and he looks after his horses well."

"They'll soon take you away," said Ginger, "and I shall lose the only friend I have, and most likely we shall never see each other again." And about a week after this I was led away.

I think my new master took as much care of us as he could. He kept many horses and carriages of different kinds for hire. Sometimes his own men drove them; sometimes the horse and carriage were let to gentlemen or ladies who drove themselves.

Hitherto I had always been driven by people who at least knew how to drive; but in this place I was to get my experience of all the kinds of bad and ignorant driving, for I was a "job horse" and was rented to all sorts of people. As I was dependable, I was more often let out to the ignorant drivers than were some of the other horses.

First there were the tight-rein drivers—those who seemed to think that all depended upon holding the reins as hard as they could. They talked about "holding a horse up," as if a horse were not made to hold himself up. Then there were the loose-rein drivers, who let the reins lie on our backs and their hands rest on their knees. Such drivers have no control over a horse if anything happens suddenly; and a horse likes a little guidance and encouragement and to know that his driver has

not gone to sleep. Besides, a careless driver makes a careless horse; Squire Gordon always kept us to our best. He said that letting a horse get into bad habits was just as cruel as spoiling a child, for both had to suffer for it afterward.

Then there was the steam-engine style of driving; these drivers were mostly people from towns, who had never had a horse of their own and who generally traveled by rail. They seemed to think that a horse was something like a steam engine, only smaller; if they paid for it, a horse was bound to go just as far, and just as fast, and with just as heavy a load as they pleased. And be the roads heavy or muddy, or dry and good, stony or smooth, uphill or downhill, it was all the same. And these drivers, instead of starting slowly, set off at full speed from the stable yard; and when they want to stop, they pull up so suddenly that we are thrown on our haunches and our mouths are jagged with the bit; and when they turn a corner, they do it as sharply as if there were no right or wrong side of the road.

Of course, we sometimes came in for good driving here. One gentle-man took a great liking to me, and after trying me several times with the saddle, convinced my master to sell me to a friend of his, who wanted a safe horse for riding. And so I was sold to Mr. Barry.

My new master hired a stable and a man named Filcher as groom. My master knew little about horses, but he wished to treat me well. He ordered the best hay and grain, and at first all was well; but after a while my feed grew meager. One afternoon he rode out into the country to see a friend of his, who said, "It seems to me, Barry, that your horse does not look so well as he did when you first had him. How do you feed him?"

My master told him. The other shook his head. "I can't say who eats your grain, my dear·fellow, but I am much mistaken if your horse gets it."

I could have told them where the oats went. My groom's little son took my grain from the feed room for the poultry and rabbits that Filcher and his wife fattened for sale; and so my master found out when, a few

mornings after this, the stable door was pushed open and a policeman walked in, holding the child tight by the arm.

My next groom was a tall, good-looking fellow; but if ever there was a humbug in the shape of a man, Alfred Smirk was he. He was the laziest, most conceited fellow I ever knew. I had a loose box and might have been very comfortable if he had not been too lazy to clean it out. Standing as I did on dirty straw, my feet grew sore. One day my feet were so bad that I made two serious stumbles with my master on my back; and so he stopped at the farrier's and asked him to see what was the matter with me. The man took up my feet one by one. "Your horse has got thrush, and badly, too. This is the sort of thing we find in foul stables which are never properly cleared out." The farrier ordered all the bedding to be taken out of my box daily and the floor to be kept very clean. With this treatment, and some medicine the farrier provided, I soon regained my health. But Mr. Barry was so disgusted at being twice deceived by his grooms that he decided to give up keeping a horse, and I was therefore sold again.

No doubt a horse fair is a very amusing place to those who have nothing to lose. At any rate, there is plenty to see: long strings of young horses; droves of shaggy little ponies; hundreds of cart horses, some of them with their long tails braided and tied with scarlet cord; and a good many like myself, highbred, but come down in the world through some accident or injury. There were some splendid animals in their prime and fit for anything; but there were also a number of poor things, broken down with overwork. These last were sad sights for a horse, who knows not but that he may come to the same state.

There was one man that I at once hoped would buy me. I knew by the way he handled me that he was used to horses; he spoke gently and his gray eyes were kind and cheerful. He offered to buy me, but the sum was too low and he was refused. A very hard, loud-voiced man came after him, and I was dreadfully afraid he would have me, for he offered a better price. But the gray-eyed man stroked me and said, "Well, I think we should suit each other," and he raised his bid. "Done," said the dealer.

My new master led me out of the fair, put a saddle on me, and we traveled steadily, till at twilight we reached London. There were streets to the right and streets to the left; I thought we should never come to the end of them. We finally turned up a narrow side street and pulled up at one of the houses. The door flew open and a young woman, followed by a little girl and an older boy, ran out. There was a very lively greeting as my rider dismounted. I was led into a comfortable, clean stall, and after a good supper I lay down, thinking I was going to be happy.

My new master's name was Jeremiah Barker, but everyone called him Jerry. Polly was his wife; Harry, their son, was twelve years old; and little Dolly was eight. They were all very fond of one another; I never knew such a merry family. It was a great treat to be petted again and talked to, and I let them see that I wished to be friendly. Polly thought I was very handsome, except for the scarred knees.

"There's no one to tell us whose fault that was," said Jerry, "and I shall give him the benefit of the doubt, for a neater stepper I never rode. We'll call him Jack, after the old one."

Jerry drove a horse cab; he owned his cab and one other horse, which he took care of himself. His other horse was a tall white animal named Captain. He was old now, but when he was young, he must have been

splendid; he told me that he had long ago belonged to an officer in the cavalry and had been in a war far overseas. Captain went out in the cab all morning. Harry came in after school to feed and water me, and in the afternoon I was put to the cab. Jerry took as much trouble to see if the collar and bridle fitted comfortably as if he had been John Manly. There was no bearing rein—what a blessing that was!

The first week of my life as a cab horse was very hard. I had never been much in London, and the noise, the hurry, and the crowds of horses, carts, and carriages that I had to make my way through made me feel anxious; but I soon found that I could trust my driver, and then I got used to the rush and bustle.

Jerry always took excellent care of us, but the best thing was that we had our Sundays for rest. We worked so hard during the week that I do not think we could have kept up to it but for that day.

One day, when I had been a cab horse for two years, our cab and many others were waiting outside one of the parks when a shabby old cab drove up beside ours. The horse was an old chestnut, with ribs that showed through the dull, dirty coat. I had been eating some hay, and the wind rolled a little wisp of it away; the poor creature put out her long, thin neck and picked it up, and then turned round and looked about for more. There was a hopeless look in the eye that I could not help noticing, and then, as I was wondering where I had seen that horse before, she said, "Black Beauty, is that you?"

It was Ginger! But how changed! The beautifully arched and glossy neck was now straight and thin; the clean legs were swollen; the face that was once so full of spirit and life was now full of suffering; and I could tell by the heaving of her sides, and her frequent cough, how bad her breathing was. It was a sad tale that she had to tell. After a twelvemonth's rest at Earlshall she was sold to a gentleman. For a

little while she got on very well, but after a longer gallop than usual the old strain returned. In this way she had changed hands several times since we had parted, but always she sank lower down.

"And so at last," said she, "I was bought by a man who keeps a number of cabs and horses and rents them out. You look well off, and I am glad of it, but I will not tell you what my life has been. When they found out that my wind was bad, they said I was not worth what they paid for me, and that I was just to be used up. That is what they are doing, working, working, working, all the week round and round, with never a Sunday rest."

I said, "You used to stand up for yourself if you were ill-used."

"Ah!" she said. "I did once, but it's no use. Men are strongest, and if they are cruel, there is nothing that we can do but just bear it, on and on to the end. I wish the end was come. I wish I was dead."

This made me very unhappy, but I could say nothing to comfort her, though she said she was pleased to see me. Just then her driver came back and, with a yank on her mouth, drove off.

A few weeks after this a cart with a dead horse in it passed us where we were waiting for a fare; the head hung out the back of the cart. I can't speak of it; the sight was too dreadful. It was a chestnut horse with a long, thin neck. I believe it was Ginger; I hoped it was, for then her troubles would be over.

My third winter as a cab horse came in early, with a great deal of cold and wet. There was snow, or sleet, almost every day for weeks. When the streets are slippery, that is the worst of all for us horses. Every nerve and muscle of our bodies is straining to keep our balance; and the fear of falling is the most exhausting of all.

Christmas and the New Year are very merry times for some people; but for cabmen and cabmen's horses it is no holiday. There are so many parties and balls that the work is hard and often late. We had a great deal of late work Christmas week, and Jerry had caught a cold and his cough was very bad. On New Year's Eve we had to take two gentlemen to a house at nine o'clock and were told to come again at eleven. As the clock struck eleven we were at the door, for Jerry was always punctual. The clock chimed the quarters, and then struck twelve, but the door did not open. The wind had been very changeable, with squalls of rain during the day, and now it turned to sharp, driving sleet, which seemed to come from all directions.

At quarter past one the door opened and the two gentlemen came out; they got into the cab without a word. My legs were numb with cold. The men never said they were sorry to have kept us waiting so long, and when they got out they were angry at the charge. They had to pay for the two hours and a quarter waiting; but it was hard-earned money to Jerry. When we got home he could hardly speak, and his cough was dreadful, but he rubbed me down as usual and even went up into the hayloft for extra straw for my bed.

It was late the next morning before anyone came, and then it was only Harry. He cleaned and fed us, but he was very quiet. At noon he came again, and Dolly came with him, and from what they said I understood that Jerry was dangerously ill. For a week or more there was great worry. At last Jerry grew better; but the doctor said that he must never go back to cab work if he wished to live to be an old man. The children talked, as they cared for us horses, about what their father and mother would do.

But one day Dolly had news. "Oh, Harry! Mother's old mistress, Mrs. Fowler, has written, and we are all to go and live near her; there is an

empty cottage with a garden. Her coachman is going away in the spring, and then she will want Father in his place."

It was quickly settled that the cab and horses should be sold as soon as possible. This was heavy news for me, for I was not young now, and three years of cab work, even under the best conditions, will wear on one, and I felt I was not the horse that I had been. Polly and the children bid me good-bye. "Poor old Jack! Dear Jack, I wish we could take you with us," Polly said. I never saw Jerry again after that New Year's Eve; and so I was led away to my new place.

I was sold to a grain dealer whom Jerry knew, and with him he thought I should have fair work. If my new master had always been there, I do not think I should have been overloaded, but there was a foreman who was always hurrying and driving everyone, and by the time I had been there three or four months, I found the work telling very much on my strength. But the heavy loads went on. Good feed and fair rest will keep one's strength under full work, but no horse can stand against over-loading, and I was so thoroughly worn out that a younger horse was bought in my place.

I was sold to another cab owner. I shall never forget this new master; he had black eyes and a hooked nose, his mouth was as full of teeth as a bulldog's, and his voice was as harsh as the grinding of cartwheels over gravel stones. His name was Nicholas Skinner. I never knew till then the utter misery a cab horse's life can be.

Skinner had a cheap set of cabs and hired drivers; he was hard on the men, and the men were hard on the horses, and in this place we had no Sunday rest. My life was now so wretched that I wished I might, like Ginger, drop down dead at my work and be out of my misery, and one day my wish very nearly came to pass.

I was at the cabstand at eight in the morning and had already done a good share of work when at noon we had to take a fare to the railway. The load was very heavy, for there was a family and all their luggage, box after box dragged up and fixed on the top of the cab; but I got along fairly till we came to a great hill. There the load and my own exhaustion were too much. I was struggling to keep on, goaded by constant use of the whip, when my feet slipped from under me, and I fell heavily to the ground on my side. The suddenness and force with which I fell beat all the breath out of my body. I lay perfectly still; indeed, I had no power to move, and I thought that now I was going to die. I heard a sort of confusion around me, loud, angry voices, but it was like a dream. Someone said, "He's dead, he'll never get up again." Some cold water

was thrown over my head and some more poured into my mouth, and something warm was thrown over me. I found my life coming back, and a kind man was patting me and encouraging me to rise. After one or two attempts I staggered to my feet and was gently led back to Skinner's stables. The next morning Skinner came with a farrier to look at me. The farrier said, "This is a case of overwork, not illness. There is a sale of horses in about ten days. If you rest him till then, you may get more than he is worth for dogs' meat, at any rate."

After ten days' rest I began to think it might be better to live than go to the dogs, and when I was taken to the sale, I held up my head and hoped for the best. At this sale I found myself in company with the old, broken-down horses, including some that it would have been merciful to shoot. I noticed an old man with a young boy by his side; they both had kind faces. The old man looked sadly at us. I saw his eye rest on me; I pricked my ears and looked at him.

"There's a horse, Willie, that has known better days."

"Poor old fellow!" said the boy.

"He might have been anything when he was young; look at the shape of his neck and shoulders. There's good breeding about that horse." He gave me a pat and I put out my nose in answer to his kindness, and the boy stroked my face.

"See, Grandpapa, how well he understands kindness. Could you not buy him?"

The old gentleman laughed. "Bless the boy! He is as horsey as his old grandfather."

"Do ask the price; I am sure he would grow young again in our meadows."

The old gentleman shook his head, but at the same time he slowly drew out his purse; and I was led behind them as they left the fair. The boy could hardly control his delight, and the old gentleman seemed to enjoy his pleasure.

Mr. Thoroughgood, for that was the name of my benefactor, gave orders that I should have plenty of food and the run of the meadow, and this treatment soon began to improve my condition and spirits. I had a good constitution, and I was never strained when I was young, so I had a better chance than horses that have worked before they come to their full strength. During the winter I grew so much better that by spring I felt quite young again.

"We must give him a little gentle work now," said Mr. Thoroughgood. "He has an excellent temperament and good paces; we must look for a quiet place where he will be valued."

One day that summer the groom cleaned me with such care that I thought some change must be at hand. A smart-looking young man came to fetch me. At first he looked pleased; but when he saw my knees, he said in a disappointed voice, "I didn't think, sir, that you would have recommended to my ladies an untrustworthy horse."

"Handsome is as handsome does," said my master. "If he is not as safe as any horse you ever drove, send him back."

I was led to a comfortable stable, fed, and left alone. The next day, when the young man was cleaning my face, he said, "That is just like the star that Black Beauty had; and this horse is much the same height, too. I wonder where he is now." A little farther on he came to a little scar on my neck. He started, and began to look me over carefully.

"White star, one white foot on the off side, this little scar in just that place"—looking at the middle of my back—"and there is that little patch of white hair. It must be Black Beauty! Why, Beauty! Do you know me? Little Joe Green who almost killed you?" He began patting me as if he was quite overjoyed.

I could not say that I remembered him, for now he was a fine-grown young fellow with black whiskers, but I was sure he knew me, and that he was Joe Green, and I was very glad. I put my nose up to him and tried to say that we were friends. "Give you a fair trial? I should think so indeed! I wonder who the rascal was that broke your knees! You must have been badly used somewhere; but it won't be my fault if you haven't a good time of it now. I wish John Manly was here to see you."

In the afternoon I was put into a low cart, for one of my new ladies wished to try me; Joe went with her, but I found that she was a good driver, and she seemed pleased with me. I heard Joe telling her about me, and that he was sure I was Squire Gordon's old Black Beauty. When we returned, the two other sisters came out to hear how I had behaved myself. She told them what she had just heard and said: "I shall write to Mrs. Gordon and tell her that her favorite horse has come to us. How pleased she will be!"

I was driven every day for a week or so, and the ladies all came to like me. After this it was decided to keep me and call me by my old name of Black Beauty.

I have now lived in this happy place a whole year. Joe is the best and kindest of grooms, and my work is easy and pleasant. Willie always speaks to me when he can and treats me as his special friend. My ladies have promised that I shall never be sold, and so I have nothing to fear; and here my story ends. My troubles are all over, and I am at home; but often, before I am quite awake, I imagine I am in Squire Gordon's orchard at Birtwick, standing with my old friends under the trees.